PowerKids Readers:

The Bilingual Library of the United States of America™

Bilingual Edition
English/Spanish
Edición bilingüe

VERMONT

JENNIFER WAY

TRADUCCIÓN AL ESPAÑOL: MARÍA CRISTINA BRUSCA

The Rosen Publishing Group's
PowerKids Press™ & **Editorial Buenas Letras**™
New York

Published in 2006 by The Rosen Publishing Group, Inc.
29 East 21st Street, New York, NY 10010

First Edition

Photo Credits: Cover © Bob Krist/Corbis; pp. 5, 25, 30 (Capital) © Joseph Sohm; ChromoSohm, Inc./Corbis; p. 7 © 2002 Geoatlas; p. 9 © James P. Blair/Corbis; pp. 11, 17, 31 (Arthur, Coolidge, von Trapp) © Bettmann/Corbis; p. 13 Library and Archives Canada/C–011724; pp. 15, 31 (Willard, Dewey) © Corbis; p. 19 © Robert Maass/Corbis; pp. 21, 31 (Skiing) © Don Mason/Corbis; p. 23 Jim Westphalen, courtesy of the Montshire Museum; pp. 26, 30 (Sugar Maple) © Robert Estall/Corbis; p. 30 (Red Clover) © Ian Rose; Frank Lane Picture Agency/Corbis; p. 30 (Hermit Thrush) © Clive Druett; Papilio/Corbis; p. 30 (The Green Mountain State) © David Muench/Corbis; p. 31 (Vallee) © Condé Nast Archive/Corbis; p. 31 (Fort) © Mark E. Gibson/Corbis; p. 31 (Syrup) © Macduff Everton/Corbis

Library of Congress Cataloging-in-Publication Data

Way, Jennifer.
Vermont / Jennifer Way ; traducción al español, María Cristina Brusca. — 1st ed.
    p. cm. — (The bilingual library of the United States of America)
Includes bibliographical references and index.
ISBN 1-4042-3111-0 (library binding)
1. Vermont—Juvenile literature. I. Title. II. Series.
F49.3.W3918 2006
974.3—dc22
                                                    2005028580

Manufactured in the United States of America

Due to the changing nature of Internet links, Editorial Buenas Letras has developed an online list of Web sites related to the subject of this book. This site is updated regularly. Please use this link to access the list:

http://www.buenasletraslinks.com/ls/vermont

Contents

Contenido

Welcome to Vermont

Vermont is the fifth-smallest state in the United States. Vermont is known as the Green Mountain State. The Green Mountains are a group of mountains that run through Vermont.

Bienvenidos a Vermont

Vermont es el quinto estado más pequeño de los Estados Unidos. Vermont es conocido como el Estado de la Montaña Verde. Las montañas Green (Verde) forman una cadena montañosa que atraviesa Vermont.

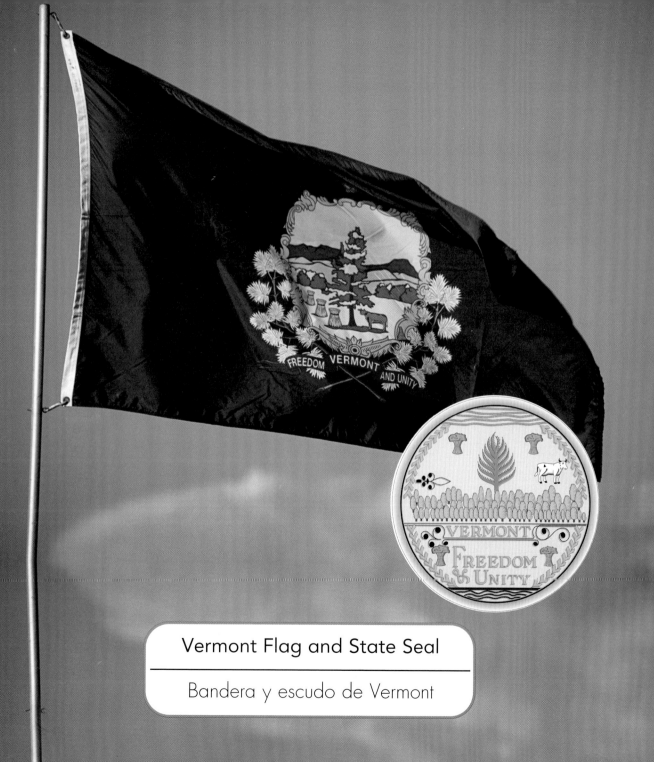

Vermont Flag and State Seal

Bandera y escudo de Vermont

Vermont Geography

Vermont is in an area known as New England. Vermont borders the states of Massachusetts, New Hampshire, and New York. Vermont also borders the country of Canada.

Geografía de Vermont

Vermont está en una región conocida como Nueva Inglaterra. Vermont linda con los estados de Massachusetts, Nuevo Hampshire y Nueva York. Vermont también linda con otro país, Canadá.

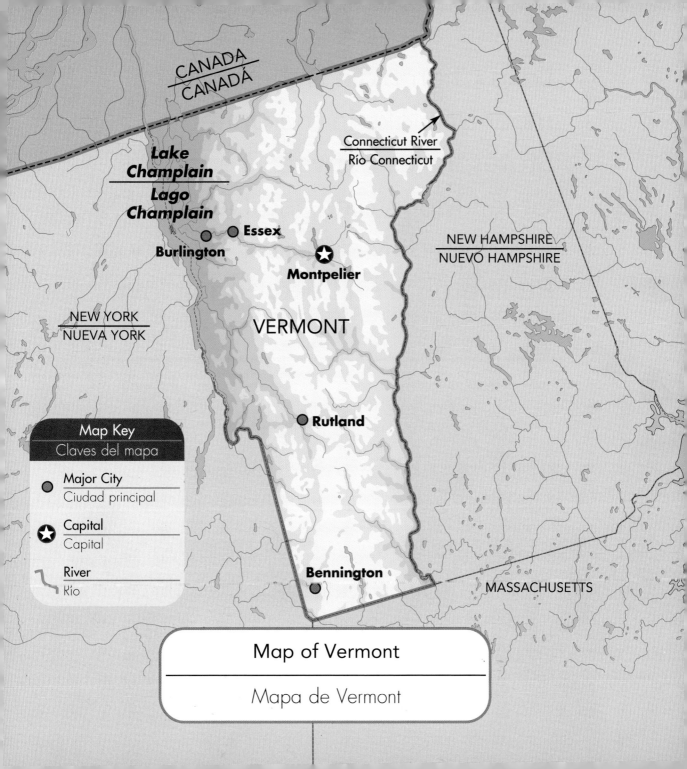

CANADA
CANADÁ

Lake
Champlain

Lago
Champlain

Connecticut River
Río Connecticut

Essex

Burlington

Montpelier

NEW HAMPSHIRE
NUEVO HAMPSHIRE

NEW YORK
NUEVA YORK

VERMONT

Rutland

Bennington

MASSACHUSETTS

Map Key
Claves del mapa

Major City
Ciudad principal

Capital
Capital

River
Río

Map of Vermont

Mapa de Vermont

Lake Champlain is the largest mountain lake in the United States. It lies between Vermont's Green Mountains and New York's Adirondack Mountains. The city of Burlington is on Lake Champlain.

El lago Champlain es el lago de montaña más grande de Estados Unidos. Está situado entre las montañas Green de Vermont y los montes Adirondack de Nueva York. La ciudad de Burlington está cerca del lago Champlain.

Lake Champlain

Lago Champlain

Vermont History

At the beginning of the American Revolution, Fort Ticonderoga was controlled by the British. American soldiers led by Vermonter Ethan Allen took over the fort in 1775.

Historia de Vermont

Al inicio de la Guerra de Independencia, el Fuerte Ticonderoga estaba controlado por los británicos. En 1775, un grupo de soldados americanos tomaron el fuerte guiados por el vermontés Ethan Allen.

Ethan Allen (1738–1789)

The Saint Albans Raid was the northernmost battle in the Civil War. On October 19, 1864, a small group of Confederate soldiers charged the town of Saint Albans and robbed its bank.

El Ataque a San Albans se considera la batalla más al norte de la Guerra Civil. El 19 de octubre de 1864 un pequeño grupo de soldados confederados atacó el pueblo de San Albans y robó su banco.

The Saint Albans Raiders

Los asaltantes de San Albans

Emma Willard worked to make education for nineteenth-century women better. At that time women were not allowed to study the same things as men were. Willard taught school in Middlebury, Vermont.

Emma Willard trabajó para mejorar la educación de las mujeres del siglo diecinueve. En aquellos tiempos a las mujeres no se les permitía estudiar las mismas cosas que a los hombres. Willard fue maestra en Middlebury, Vermont.

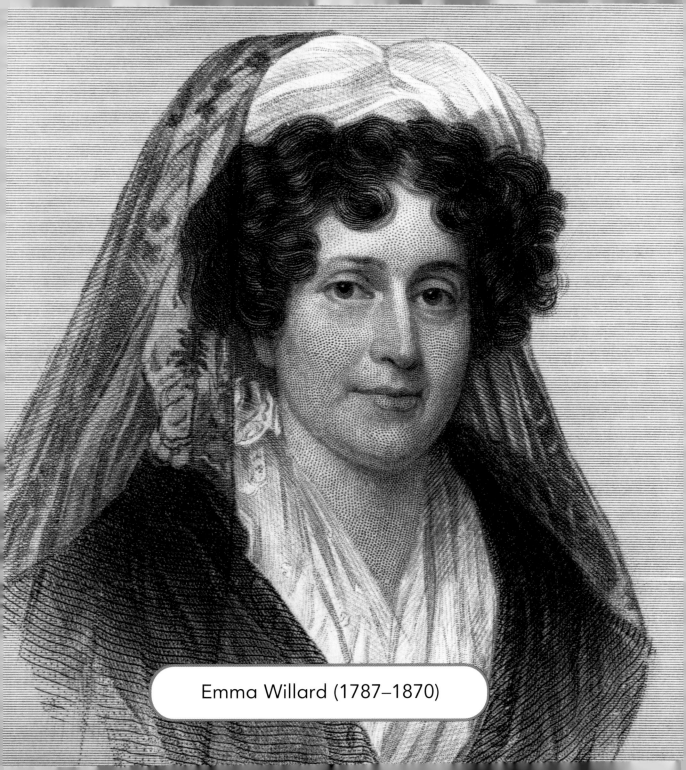

Emma Willard (1787–1870)

Calvin Coolidge was born in Plymouth Notch in 1872. Coolidge was the thirtieth president of the United States. He served from 1923 to 1929. His nickname was "Silent Cal" because he did not talk very much.

Calvin Coolidge nació en Plymouth Notch en 1872. Coolidge fue el trigésimo presidente de los Estados Unidos. Gobernó de 1923 a 1929. Como no hablaba mucho recibió el sobrenombre de "El Mudo Cal".

Calvin Coolidge (1873–1933)

Living in Vermont

Vermont is famous for its maple syrup. Each spring maple trees are tapped, and the tree sap flows into buckets. The sap is then made into maple syrup.

La vida en Vermont

Vermont es famoso por su jarabe de arce (maple). Cada primavera se perforan los arces y la savia de los árboles se recoge en baldes. Con la savia se elabora el jarabe.

Gathering Sap in Vermont

Recolección de savia en Vermont

Every winter many visitors come to the mountains of Vermont. Skiing is a popular winter sport in Vermont. Many Olympic athletes who have won medals for skiing are from Vermont.

En el invierno las montañas de Vermont reciben muchos visitantes. El esquí es un deporte invernal muy popular en Vermont. Muchos campeones olímpicos de esquí son originarios de Vermont.

Cross-country Skiing in Vermont

Práctica de esquí de fondo en Vermont

Vermont Today

The Montshire Museum of Science has lots of fun exhibits where you can learn about science. It also has an outdoor science park where you can study the river and the wildlife.

Vermont, hoy

En el Museo de Ciencia Montshire hay muchas exhibiciones para aprender acerca de la ciencia. También hay un parque científico al aire libre donde puedes estudiar el río y la vida silvestre.

The Montshire Museum of Science in Norwich

Museo de Ciencia Montshire en Norwich

Burlington, Essex, Rutland, and Bennington are the biggest cities in Vermont. Montpelier is the capital of the state of Vermont.

Burlington, Essex, Rutland y Bennington son las ciudades más grandes de Vermont. Montpelier es la capital del estado de Vermont.

The Vermont State Capitol in Montpelier

Capitolio del estado de Vermont, en Montpelier

Activity:
Let's draw Vermont's State Tree
The sugar maple became Vermont's state tree in 1929.

Actividad:
Dibujemos el árbol del estado de Vermont
El arce azucarero es el árbol del estado de Vermont desde 1929.

1

Draw two lines that come to a point at the top. This is the trunk.

Dibuja dos líneas que se junten arriba, en un punto. Éste es el tronco.

2

Lightly draw a big cloud shape over the tree. Turn your pencil on its side and lightly shade this area.

Dibuja suavemente, sobre el tronco, una forma parecida a una nube. Luego, tomando el lápiz de costado, sombrea con suavidad esta zona.

3

Shape the tree by erasing some of the cloud shape from step 2. Next press the tip of your pencil to shade little dark patches where the leaves would be.

Dale forma al árbol borrando algunas partes de la forma de nube que dibujaste en el paso 2. Luego, apretando la punta del lápiz, sombrea pequeñas áreas oscuras donde quieras las hojas.

4

Fill in the tree's trunk. Now define the tree's branches. Good job!

Rellena el tronco del árbol. Ahora dibuja las ramas. ¡Buen trabajo!

Timeline

Cronología

French explorer Jacques Cartier is the first European to see Vermont.	**1535**	El explorador francés Jacques Cartier es el primer europeo en avistar Vermont.
The first European settlement, Fort Sainte Anne, is built by the French on Isle La Motte.	**1666**	El fuerte Sainte Anne, primer establecimiento europeo, es construído por los franceses en Isle La Motte.
Vermont's constitution is the first in the United States to outlaw the practice of slavery.	**1777**	La constitución de Vermont es la primera de los Estados Unidos en declarar ilegal la esclavitud.
Vermont is the fourteenth state to join the United States.	**1791**	Vermont es el decimocuarto estado en unirse a los Estados Unidos.
Montpelier becomes the capital of Vermont.	**1805**	Montpelier se convierte en la capital de Vermont.
John Deere invents the steel plow.	**1837**	John Deere inventa el arado de acero.
The first Boy Scout club in America is formed in Barre.	**1909**	Se forma el primer club Boy Scout de América, en Barre.
Madeleine Kuni becomes Vermont's first woman governor.	**1984**	Madeleine Kuni llega a ser la primera gobernadora de Vermont.

Vermont Events	Eventos en Vermont
January	Enero
Stowe Winter Carnival in Stowe	Carnaval de invierno de Stowe, en Stowe
March	Marzo
Vermont Flower Show in Burlington	Exposición floral, en Burlington
Whitingham Maple Festival in Whitingham	Festival del arce, en Whitingham
June	Junio
Vermont Dairy Festival in Enosburg Falls	Festival de los productos lácteos de Vermont, en Enosburg Falls
August	Agosto
Orleans County Fair in Barton	Feria del condado de Orleans, en Barton
Vermont Mozart Festival in Stowe	Festival Mozart de Vermont, en Stowe
Champlain Valley Exposition in Essex Junction	Exposición del Valle Champlain, en Essex Junction
Native American Powwow in Evansville	Powwow nativoamericano, en Evansville
September	Septiembre
Vermont State Fair in Rutland	Feria del estado de Vermont, en Rutland
Stowe Oktoberfest in Stowe	Oktoberfest de Stowe, en Stowe
October	Octubre
Vermont Sheep and Wool Festival in Essex Junction	Festival de la oveja y la lana de Vermont, en Essex Junction
November	Noviembre
Winter Festival of Vermont Crafters in Barre	Festival invernal de artesanía vermontés, en Barre

29

Vermont Facts/Datos sobre Vermont

<table>
<tr>
<td>

Population
608,827

</td>
<td></td>
<td>

Población
608,827

</td>
</tr>
<tr>
<td>

Capital
Montpelier

</td>
<td></td>
<td>

Capital
Montpelier

</td>
</tr>
<tr>
<td>

State Motto
Freedom and Unity

</td>
<td></td>
<td>

Lema del estado
Libertad y unidad

</td>
</tr>
<tr>
<td>

State Flower
Red clover

</td>
<td></td>
<td>

Flor del estado
Trébol rojo

</td>
</tr>
<tr>
<td>

State Bird
Hermit thrush

</td>
<td></td>
<td>

Ave del estado
Zorzal ermitaño

</td>
</tr>
<tr>
<td>

State Nickname
The Green Mountain State

</td>
<td></td>
<td>

Mote del estado
El Estado de la Montaña Verde

</td>
</tr>
<tr>
<td>

State Tree
Sugar maple

</td>
<td></td>
<td>

Árbol del estado
Arce azucarero

</td>
</tr>
<tr>
<td>

State Song
"Those Green Mountains"

</td>
<td></td>
<td>

Canción del estado
"Aquellas montañas verdes"

</td>
</tr>
</table>

Famous Vermonters/Vermonteses famosos

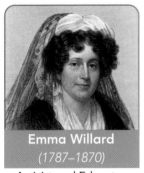
Emma Willard
(1787–1870)
Activist and Educator
Activista y educadora

Chester A. Arthur
(1829–1886)
U.S. president
Presidente de E.U.A.

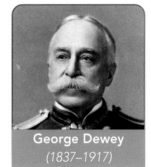
George Dewey
(1837–1917)
U.S. Navy admiral
Almirante de E.U.A.

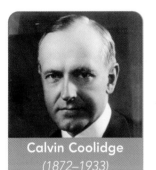
Calvin Coolidge
(1872–1933)
U.S. president
Presidente de E.U.A.

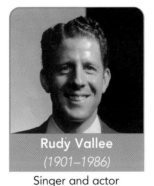
Rudy Vallee
(1901–1986)
Singer and actor
Cantante y actor

Maria von Trapp
(1905–1987)
Singer
Cantante

Words to Know/Palabras que debes saber

border
frontera

fort
fuerte

skiing
esquiar

syrup
jarabe

Here are more books to read about Vermont:
Otros libros que puedes leer sobre Vermont:

In English/En inglés:

Vermont
by Ann Heinrichs
Children's Press, 2001

M Is for Maple Syrup: A Vermont Alphabet
by Cynthia Furlong Reynolds
Sleeping Bear Press, 2002

Words in English: 323   Palabras en español: 346

Index

Índice